TEDDY

THE **REMARKABLE** TALE OF A **PRESIDENT**,
A **CARTOONIST**, A **TOYMAKER** AND A **BEAR**

JAMES SAGE · LISK FENG

KIDS CAN PRESS

Theodore Roosevelt, or T.R. to his friends, was once president of the United States.

When he wasn't too busy running the country, he liked to

ride horses

wrestle

read

lift weights

write books

sail boats

play football

give speeches

go camping

go hunting

But not all at the same time.

One year, his presidential duties took him south, to the state of Mississippi. Between arranging treaties and other such things, he went hunting.

His hosts had hoped he might bag a bear or two. But word that T.R. was coming must have spread quickly, for soon there wasn't a bear to be seen for miles around ...

... except, that is, for one scruffy, no-account cub.

"Me? Shoot that little fella?" said the president. "Why, if I so much as ruffled his fur, I'd never be able to look my children in the eyes again!"

So he put away his gun and returned to Washington and his home in the White House — and that was the end of that.

Except that it wasn't.

For in another part of the city, in the very busy offices of its most important newspaper, the staff cartoonist, Mr. Clifford Berryman, was being visited by his editor in chief.

"Clifford, I want something different, something that touches the heart ... something that speaks to everyone. Have your cartoon on my desk first thing in the morning. WITHOUT FAIL."

"Yes, sir. No problem at all, sir. Without fail, sir."

Yet, there *was* a problem. A very big problem.
He couldn't think of anything to draw!
"I have an idea," said Harry, the coffee boy,
who was always hanging around the newsroom.
He told Mr. Berryman about the president
and the cub. The story had just come in over the
newswire.

"That's the ticket!" said Mr. Berryman, with a smile of relief. "Young man, you've saved the day! Here, have a doughnut, on me."

He drew all night, and as the sun rose over the waking city, he put the finishing touches to his cartoon.

"Excellent! Excellent!" said his editor in chief, between puffs on his cigar. "I've got to hand it to you, Clifford, you sure know how to draw bears. Yessiree, that's one cuddly bear cub all right."

Others thought so, too. The cartoon was reprinted in newspaper after newspaper, in every town and city in the land ... including Brooklyn, New York, where a Mr. and Mrs. Michtom had a little shop. They sold newspapers and candy, novelties and stationery and even, sometimes, Mrs. Michtom's handmade toys.

"Rosie! Rosie! Take a look at this — the president of the United States refusing to shoot a little bear. Can you beat that!"

"He should be so lucky, Morris. Not every bear gets to meet the president."

"But such a president, Rosie! We must let everyone know what a big warm heart he has."

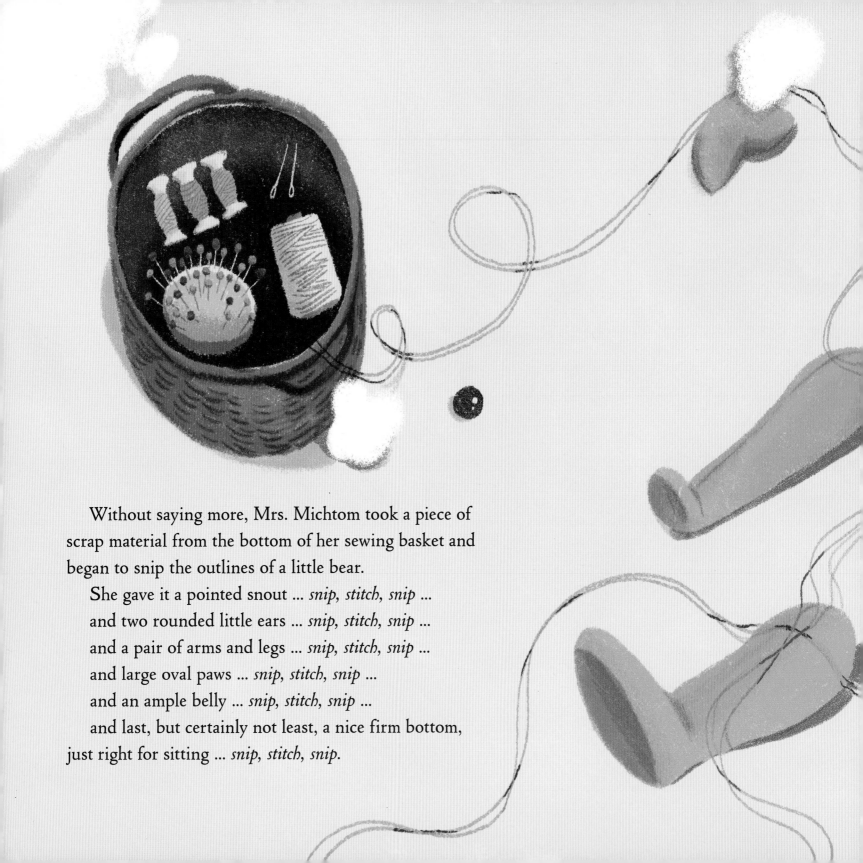

Without saying more, Mrs. Michtom took a piece of scrap material from the bottom of her sewing basket and began to snip the outlines of a little bear.

She gave it a pointed snout ... *snip, stitch, snip* ...
and two rounded little ears ... *snip, stitch, snip* ...
and a pair of arms and legs ... *snip, stitch, snip* ...
and large oval paws ... *snip, stitch, snip* ...
and an ample belly ... *snip, stitch, snip* ...
and last, but certainly not least, a nice firm bottom, just right for sitting ... *snip, stitch, snip*.

Then she stitched it all together and stuffed it carefully with fine wood shavings, the same she used for all her toys.

"What will you do for eyes, my dear?" asked Mr. Michtom, who had been watching her with interest.

"Your black shoe buttons will do nicely, Morris. I'll get you new ones tomorrow."

"And don't forget the nose," added Mr. Michtom. "A bear's not a bear without his sniffly snout."

But Mrs. Michtom had thought of that, too. She chose some strong darning thread from her sewing basket and stitched on a little black nose.

"There now," she said, holding up the bear for inspection. "What do you think?"

Mr. Michtom was delighted. "We'll put it in the shop window, Rosie, near the front for all to see. And we'll add a sign, too."

But just then, Mr. Michtom thought of something else — something very important.

TEDDY'S BEAR

AS PORTRAYED BY THE FAMOUS ARTIST,
MR. CLIFFORD K. BERRYMAN

"Perhaps we had better ask permission to use the president's name in advertising our bear, my dear. After all, 'Teddy' Roosevelt is president of the United States."

So Mr. Michtom hauled a stool over to the counter, sat down and wrote the president of the United States a letter.

When the president received it, he stopped whatever he was doing at that moment, which was no doubt quite important, and dashed off a reply:

WHITE HOUSE
WASHINGTON

Dear Mr. Michtom:

While I don't expect my name will do much good selling bears, you are welcome to use it as you have indicated. It is a BULLY idea!

Sincerely yours,

Theodore Roosevelt, President

P.S. Written in haste!

"Only in America!" said Mr. Michtom,
beaming proudly.
    "And on White House stationery, yet," said
Mrs. Michtom.

It wasn't long before it seemed everyone in America wanted to own a teddy bear (for the name had stuck)!

There were teddy bears dressed as

cowboys,
bellhops,
train conductors,
undersea divers,
clowns,
cricketers,
fox hunters
and schoolboys.

There were

Boy Scouts,
hospital patients,
chefs,
mechanics,
soldiers,
sailors
and aviators.

There were teddy bears made of

burlap,
calico,
velvet,
flannel,
mohair,
wool
and alpaca.

There were

brown teddy bears,
black teddy bears,
auburn teddy bears,
white teddy bears,
golden teddy bears

and even a red teddy bear, ordered by a Russian grand duke for his daughter, Princess Xenia.

And to go with all these teddy bears, there were

teddy bear wardrobes,
teddy bear steamer trunks,
teddy bear tea sets,
teddy bear books,
teddy bear songs,
teddy bear games
and, of course, plenty of teddy bear picnic baskets.

The world was filling up with teddy bears! And still there was a demand for more.

Mr. and Mrs. Michtom were so overwhelmed with orders they had to close their little corner shop and build a big factory — a really big factory entirely devoted to the making of teddy bears — which they called the Ideal Novelty and Toy Company.

From its vast assembly lines, teddy bears tumbled forth, twenty-four hours a day, week after week after week ... hundreds and thousands and millions of teddy bears of every description, size and shape.

Yet, as different as they all were — even
the ones that were supposed to be exactly the
same — they all had one thing in common ...

"You know, Rosie," said Mr. Michtom,
"I think the reason kids love teddy bears so
much is that they're so darn cuddly."

"Oh, no, my dear," Mrs. Michtom said, "it's because teddy bears give cuddles in return."

And there wasn't anyone anywhere who could possibly disagree.

Not even the president.

AUTHOR'S NOTE

Teddy blends fact with fiction to tell the story of the creation of the first teddy bear.

For example, whether the cartoonist, Clifford Berryman, shared his doughnuts with the coffee boy is pure conjecture — although I would like to think he did. And whether the Michtoms liked cuddles, with or without a teddy bear, is again pleasant speculation on my part.

Myths have always been a way of explaining what cannot be easily explained or understood otherwise. For this reason, it seemed a useful way of relaying why the teddy bear was such a success. Here was an object to which millions could confide their hopes and dreams and secrets. Here was a little bear that not only received love, but offered it in return many times over.

Is it any wonder, then, that this most iconic of companions would become one of the most endearing companions of modern times?

The original cartoon by Clifford Berryman, first published in the Washington Post *on November 16, 1902*

When Theodore Roosevelt, affectionately known as "T.R." or "Teddy," was president of the United States (1901–1909), he was invited to go bear hunting in the state of Mississippi. Having always loved the outdoor life, he accepted with pleasure. But on this occasion, he didn't find any bears. His hosts, not wanting T.R. to leave disappointed, finally tracked down a bear and tied it to a tree for the president to shoot. But T.R. refused to kill it, believing it would be unsportsmanlike. So he returned to Washington, D.C. empty-handed, but with his honor very much intact.

When this news reached the office of cartoonist Clifford Berryman, it was decided his newspaper would portray the incident in the form of a political cartoon. It was an instant success. The public was charmed by this display of sportsmanship and compassion, and Berryman's cartoon was reprinted in newspapers across the country and around the world.

The story of the president's refusal to shoot a bear sparked the imagination of Morris and Rose Michtom. Rose made a toy bear, which they displayed in the window of their candy shop with the name "Teddy's Bear." According to some reports, Morris wrote to the president to ask permission to use his nickname, and the Michtom family has said that the president wrote back; however, no one has found either letter.

One of the first teddy bears produced by the Ideal Novelty & Toy Company (c. 1903)

Rose's toy bears became so popular the Michtoms opened a factory named the Ideal Novelty & Toy Company just a year later, in 1903.

The facing photo shows a very early example of a teddy bear, made by the Michtoms' company. It is one of the most popular displays in the Smithsonian National

Museum of American History in Washington. It was donated to the museum by descendants of Theodore Roosevelt. In newspapers, the president was often portrayed in the company of bears, a gentle nod to the bear he refused to shoot.

A page advertising the "Original" teddy bear from the Ideal Novelty & Toy Company catalog, 1950. Landauer GV1219. I44 1950, New-York Historical Society Library, 96676d.

The above image shows an early advertisement for teddy bears from the Ideal Novelty & Toy Company. The bear in the photo is shown seated rather than standing, the result of an invention by a German company, Steiff, that had also been producing plush bears and other animals around the time the Michtoms created their first teddy bear. The arms and legs of the bear could now be made to move freely, allowing it to be set in more than one position. This important innovation was eventually incorporated into most teddy bears, adding greatly to their popularity.

For Ann — J.S.
For Jinxian Zhang, my grandmother — L.F.

Kids Can Press gratefully acknowledges the financial support of the Government of Ontario, through the Ontario Media Development Corporation.

Published in Canada and the U.S. by Kids Can Press Ltd.
25 Dockside Drive, Toronto, ON M5A 0B5

Kids Can Press is a Corus Entertainment Inc. company

www.kidscanpress.com

The artwork in this book was rendered digitally.
The text is set in Cloister URW.

Edited by Yasemin Uçar
Designed by Julia Naimska and Andrew Dupuis

Printed and bound in Malaysia in 10/2018 by Tien Wah Press (Pte.) Ltd.

CM 19 0 9 8 7 6 5 4 3 2 1

Library and Archives Canada Cataloguing in Publication

Sage, James, author
     Teddy : the remarkable tale of a president, a cartoonist, a toymaker and a bear / James Sage.

Illustrated by Lisk Feng.

ISBN 978-1-77138-795-8 (hardcover)

     I. Feng, Lisk, illustrator II. Title.

PZ7.S234Ted 2019   j813'.54   C2018-903612-5

Photo credits

Every reasonable effort has been made to trace ownership of and give accurate credit to copyrighted material. Information that would enable the publisher to correct any discrepancies in future editions would be appreciated.

p. 38: Berryman family papers, 1829–1984, (bulk 1882–1961). Archives of American Art, Smithsonian Institution

p. 39 (left): Division of Political History, National Museum of American History, Smithsonian Institution

p. 39 (right): New-York Historical Society